Frederick C. Bonnett

Silver Threads

In rhyme and song

Frederick C. Bonnett

Silver Threads
In rhyme and song

ISBN/EAN: 9783337271992

Printed in Europe, USA, Canada, Australia, Japan

Cover: Foto ©Andreas Hilbeck / pixelio.de

More available books at **www.hansebooks.com**

SILVER THREADS

IN

RHYME AND SONG,
ETC.

BY

D. C. BONNETT.

SILVER THREADS

—IN—

RHYME AND SONG,

—OR—

A YOUTH'S BRIEF RAMBLES
IN THE FIELD OF

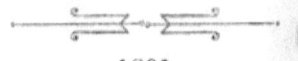

BY FREDERICK CARL BONNETT.

1891.
GAZETTE PRINTING HOUSE
MAHAFFEY, PA.

PREFACE.

In putting this small volume of poems before the reader I have no apology to offer; but the variety of subjects treated is the result of deep thought long and patiently persisted in: and it has been carefully considered and revised before going to press.

The work is not claimed to be perfect, but thoroughness and a desire to instruct, benfit and please has been my aim.

Everything is written in plain English, and may be read and easily understood by old and young.

That every reader may gather a few Silver threads from its pages is my earnest desire.

Respectfully yours.

F. C. BONNETT.

In all kind nature is revealed
  A greater power than man can wield;
Yet from man's mind great thoughts will spring
  Which tunes all nations' tongues to sing.

The growing grain, the blooming flower,
  Speak of God's wondrous love and power:
Though man is weak, his thoughts may rise
  Far up beyond the starry skies.

MORTAL LIFE.

Why should ye mortals be so proud
In this vain world of strife ?
Where joyfulness and peace is found
And vice and wickedness abound;
The stage of man we must pursue
Which is so varied and untrue.
Yet history tells us all along
The deeds of men in prose and song.
Long, long ago for ages past
The world was dreary, wild and vast.
We learn that our first parents were
Perfect and sinless without care.
Until the evil tempter came
And put them both to guilt and shame;
And thus a hiding place they sought.
They knew in sin they had been caught.
And from that self-same day we know
O'er earth men wandered to and fro.
As foul a deed as e'er was done
Was by our very first born son.
Who slew his brother that he died.
And then unto the Lord he lied.
The same as men will nowadays.
Who have so many curious ways.
Since man fell from love and grace
His devious path is hard to trace.

It leads o'er thorny, rocky ways,
Through dark, through bright and happy days,
And joys and pleasure everywhere
Fills man with many a thought and care.
Man has a body and a mind,
Is sometimes rude and sometimes kind.
There are two ways which he may tread,
One leads to life and one to death.
The one is strewn with weeds and thorns
And vicious beasts with deadly horns,
With Golden serpents everywhere
Who seek the youthful to ensnare.
The other leads to endless bliss
Where joy in great perfection is.
Along a road all strewn with flowers,
With balmy breeze and scented showers,
Where crystal springs of water clear
Will fainting spirits always cheer,
And lead them on with courage new
To join the King so good and true.
"Man is a creature born of lust,
His body will return to dust;"
His evil thought and vain desire
Can ne'er to noble things aspire;
But all his purer thoughts may rise
Until they reach beyond the skies,
A nobler, brighter world above
Where all is happiness and love.

JOHN AND JIM.
A FABLE.

Two friendly travelers, John and Jim,
Were going through the city's din.
The streets were narrow, black and cold
And busy men came through the fold.
When Jim replied ''I know a place
Where gold in great abundance lays
So let us hie in rapid haste
Unto the spot where the gold lays.
John said naught while on their way
Until the spot before them lay.
Jim got the gold and said the prize
Belonged to him alone.
Thus through the city back they went
Where thieves and robbers lay.
''Oh! John,'' says Jim ''we'd better flee
Or else for gold we'll murdered be.''
''Not we,'' says John ''but you alone,
For I can fly without a groan.''
And nimbly then his way he goes
And soon is safe from deadly foes.
But Jim bewildered and amazed
Is by the robbers quickly chased.
Is caught and robbed of all his gold
And sent away with many a scold.
He's sorely beaten by the thieves
And now o'er his selfishness he grieves.

MORAL.

Now heed the moral of this tale.
Though it concerns you not.
If much good luck fall in your hands.
Share with your friends the happy lot.
Then if ill fate should come to you.
Your faithful friends will help you through.
So be not like this hero was,
And claim all as your own.
For when in trouble you are found
Your friends will all be gone.

DISAPPOINTED.

The morn was not so bright as we do often see
In summer when the sun climbs o'er the eastern hills.
When song birds warble forth their merry notes of pleasure
In orchard. meadow. woodland. field and glen;
But rain in torrents poured from the cold and angry clouds
As morn was breaking o'er the far and distant land.
The wind was raging fiercely through the forest pine
As I was going through the field to make up precious time.
But still the rain in sheets poured on my back.
That I was loathe to shrink, but lo! alack!
I was detemined to be gone, no matter what betide.

A friend of mine, whose house I had to pass.
Went with me to the institution of a secret order lodge.
We started for a village to take the early morning train.

But when we arrived there the train had long since gone;
We cussed a little, but twas all of no avail,
So we persuaded others to join our happy band,
So there were four of us when the noon train we boarbed,
All bound for Punxy town.

While there we took some oysters for our dinner,
And washed it down ah! yes, twas nothing strong,
A friend of ours was lavish and bought us juice of hops,
And we drank all of us a hearty fill.
Next a few flasks containing Juice of Rye,
And one filled with the sap of yellow corn,
So with gay hearts and lighter steps we went
With speed o'er muddy country roads and grassy fields across;
Till we came to Covode a pleasant country town,
Where in a store the people had assembled us to see.

We were but in the store a few short minutes
When the whole truth to us was publicly revealed,
No dispensation for the institution they received,
Nor had their billy goat arrived in time,
So we our disappointment quietly did bear
And consolation in the corn juice then did take.

Our stay was short but still we viewed the hall
Where the honored K. of P. were all to be installed,
So six miles back to Punxs'y we retraced
Our steps with rapid strides through mud and field,
Until we reached a house all built of brick.
Our maws were empty and were craving food.

So in the house our chieftain we did send.
And coming forth again brought three large tempting pies.
Which, by the roadside, we did eagerly devour.

Another house was entered, but of no avail,
Nor could we get enough of straw to make a decent meal.
So wearily again we plod our way.
Until we came to town, where straightway we did go
Into a hotel where a dainty meal was spread for supper,
Which only half our hungry appetites appeased.

We went to bed and tore a sheet asunder.
And in the morn, a hearty breakfast got.
We loafed through town until our train was due.
And bade goodby to all our disappointed woe.
When on our homeward journey we were bound,
'Twas fraught with gayety took in a lighter sense,
But then our pocket books were out a host of cents.

MORNING SLEEP.

INFINITUDE and temporary bliss,
How sweet the sleep of peace and health
'That's gained by sleeping early in the morn,
When launched in dreamland, oh! so happy then,
Relieved from sorrow and from worldly care,
Oblivious of the duties of the coming day,
Or future prospects that before us lie,
Being well contented with present environments.

Awake, arise and stir yourself about.
Improve those precious moments in the morn;
Behold the eastern sun ascending high
O'er yonder pearly mountains decked with dew.
Look in the stream and rivulet that sparkle,
Reflecting all the glory in the morning sun.
Live in those scenes and be inspired with life and vigor fresh,
And see to all the cares and duties of the day.

LAZY JAKE.

WHERE once was a boy, his name was Jake.
He was so lazy, O, dear, sake!
He wouldn't bring a stick of wood,
If he had to do without his food.

He wallowed in the dirt and mud
And then came in the house to fuss,
He sat behind the cooking stove
And watched the hens and Turkey's roast

Poor Jake would often, often cry,
If he got a little piece of pie;
But when the biggest piece he got
He was so happy that he'd trot.

He didn't like to go to school,
To Sunday school or church:
But always played on Sunday morn.
Until the hour of church was gone.

ALL IN A SPLUTTER.

NOW what do you think many a woman will do,
  When all in a splutter to get her work through
Because a new show exhibits in town,
  And she would not miss it to save half a crown ?

In her haste she upsets the table and chairs
  And falls o'er the baby, that is coming down stairs,
And meets the hard floor with a good hearty thump,
  But then it's all right, she is up in a jump.

She seeks for her coat, her gloves, and her shawl,
  While the baby comes running and terribly bawls;
But she does not heed it, but looks for her hat,
  And in her turmoil she tramps on the cat.

The cat gives a sorrowful heart-rending scream.
  In running and jumping it falls in the cream;
And a spectacle, white, all dripping and wet,
  The baby's amusement, and white household pet.

But by and by the mistress gets calm.
  To be at the show is her sweet healing balm.
So she runs to a neighbor and borrows a hat,
  And at last she is off with a rat tat tat.

The cream and the chairs are all on the floor.
  The cats and the dogs are happy once more:
But she is enjoying herself at the show,
  And when she comes home what sorrow and woe.

WORLDLY CHARMS.

THIS world possesses many charms.
  And many cultivated farms:
So many things so bright and fair,
  Which makes the keen-eyed wand'er stare.

The peaceful hours which here we spend,
  But for a time to us are lent:
While warmth of heat and burning light
  Will make a gloomy spirit bright.

Those charms that oft' attract us so
  Are full of misery and woe:
Our pleasures here will soon have an end,
  No matter how our life is spent.

The charms of peace will not decay,
  Which we enjoy from day to day.
Our deeds will always, always stand,
  If judged by the Supreme command.

Prosperity we here can find,
  With knowledge true store up our minds.
Our troubles and cares are meted out,
  While riches but by few are found.

The charms and glitter of silver and gold
  Will vanish away and turn into mould;
But charms that are priceless and flow from the heart
  Should ne'er be rejected, nor ne'er from us part.

COMING OF SPRING.

THE winter will soon be over.
    And cold winds will cease to **blow**:
The frost will come out of the **trees**,
    And the ground desert all its snow.

The ice will melt on the streams
    And frogs will dance on their shores;
And fishermen know it is time
    To catch the good fishes **once more.**

The trees will be covered with leaves,
    And the meadows all green with grass;
The apple and the cherry trees bloom
    So lovely and grand as we pass.

The woods will be strewn with nice flowers
    So beautiful lovely and fair
And bees a-buzzing will go
    And gather sweet honey so rare.

SUMMER RAMBLINGS.

I love to ramble in the woods
  On pleasant summer days,
And view the scenes that nature gives
  In all her charming ways.

I love to ramble by the brook,
  Or by the lone sea-side;
And view the ocean, vast **and grand**,
  Which reaches far and wide.

I love the fragrance of the flowers
  That grow down in the dell,
Whose odors sweet and **rich perfume**
  Are pleasant to the smell.

I love to fish down by the stream,
  Where shady trees do stand;
And catch the little finny tribe
  And put them on dry land.

I love to **ramble where the rose**
  And flowers bloom so **fair**;
Where mossy greens and buttercups
  Grow without thought or **care**.

I love to **see** the birds that sing
  Their joyful morning song,
To hear the thunder as it **rolls**
  In peals both loud and long.

I love to see harmonious **peace**
  Through all the seasons **sound**.
And like the calm mild summer days
  Love always should be found.

SUMMER HOURS.

HOW brightly shines the sun
  O'er mountains, hills and **vales**;
How green is all the meadow land
  Where lambs do skip and play.

The yellow **grain** fields we behold
  So lovely to our sight;
We see the reapers willing hands,
  Work hard from morn till night.

Tis **pleasant in the** woods to roam,
  Where small fresh streamlets flow,
We hear the merry song of **birds**,
  As we go to and fro.

So we should always do our best,
  While summer hours last,
And make the **present** always **bright**,
  And all forgive the past.

SWEET MEMORIES.

I WELL do remember in years that are gone.
To think of the past makes me feel sad and lone;
Yet the past has a charm a sweet lingering charm
    Which time and ages can never disarm.

When we think of the days, those innocent days,
    When nothing beclouded our childish ways;

While to day we are wandering to the grave yard once more
    The medium of life and eternity's shore.

My recollections far back I often have cast,
    'Tis sad and sweet to think of the past;
How neglectful in goodness and kindness we were,
    When we were all free from trouble and care.

I have often wept over memory's page,
    Shed tears of joy o'er the grave of the sage;

I've planted bright flowers o'er the small grassy mound
Where rest the dear friends neath the dreary cold ground.

LITTLE BY LITTLE.

LITTLE by little progress we make,
Little by little our minds will awake
To prospects of greatness, honor and fame.
That much besides pleasure, for us is to gain.

Little by little the forest trees grow,
Steadily at it, though progress is slow;
Yet in hundreds of years they become very high.
Their majestic tops looking up to the sky.

Little by little the school boy said,
Little by little my knowledge ill get,
Little by little I'll soon be a man,
So I'll cheerily do the best that I can.

Little by little inventions are made,
    While science is willing to lend all her aid.
Little by little our cities are built
And little by little our store-house is filled.

PERSEVERANCE.

BY perseverance our ends we obtain.
    If our atm is good we should never complain:
But work with hand, with head and with heart.
    And to others the good and truthful impart.

When a task is hard let duty not shirk,
    But persevere on in your grand noble work;
Until your labors are crowned with success,
    While others, less firm, are lost in distress.

Labor on with ambition, as time passes by.
    Don't say "I can't." You don't know till you try.
To accomplish great deeds you must slowly press on.
    For sluggards have ne'er great accomplishments won.

Persevere in your your work, and sure you'll succeed.
    Sometimes rather slow, yet oft with great speed.
High honors are won by the true and the great,
    Who never sit down to rest in the shade.

A RIVULET.

The rivulet dances gaily along,
  Merrily singing its cheerful song;
Winding its course through meadow and lea,
  Steadily flowing on to the sea.

Out through the forest without any delay,
  On its gree shores young children will play;
Bathe in its water on a warm summer day
  While the sun reflecteth back its bright ray.

Hither the traveler weary and worn
  Comes to drink in the bright early morn;
The beasts of the field and fowls' of the air,
  For bright sparkling water hither repair.

What blessings and comfort nature did give,
  Providing for all that have life to live,
Those beautiful scenes that enshroud this fair land,
  We all should enjoy as we go hand in hand.

Like a serpent the rivulet laid out its path.
  Sometimes it is gentle, sometimes full of wrath,
But still it goes on so happy and free
  Until it joins the fathomless sea.

JACK IN THE CORNFIELD.

JACK, in the cornfield worked all day,
Never allowed a minute to play.
He followed the corn rows neath the hot burning sun,
While in his toil he had little fun.

He pulled out the weeds that were six inches high,
And sometimes the soil flew up in his eye;
Yet he worked all day with an old rusty hoe,
While the wind through his whiskers freely did blow

Though he worked with a will, he lamented his fate,
For weeding and hoeing poor Jackie did hate;
So he said: "I will rest neath this large shady tree,
And leave everything go merry and free."

He soon was asleep, and bright visions did pass
Before Jackie's mind as he lay in the grass.
He dreamt that in lands that are fairer than this,
He dwelt in happiness, pleasure and bliss.

But soon he awoke and stirred him about,
When he saw where he was he began for to pout,
For he saw that his indolence brought him no grain,
And in his heart he wished it would rain.

THE HOUSEWIFE.

THE housewife is busy and worketh with care.
　Of trouble and sorrow she gets her full share.
She plods·in the kitchen from morn' until night.
　.She works in the dawn and the slow fading light.

She baketh the bread and prepares the rare dish
　Of beefsteak and mutton, oysters and fish.
She fries the potatoes and stirreth the mush.
　Her face is all smiles when she does not blush.

She keeps herself neat. so tidy and trim;
　While her bright sparkling eyes some day will grow dim.
She welcomes her husband, who comes from his work.
　In her bright sunny bower no duty she shirks.

She is pleasant to all, yet duty ere pleasure.
　Who has such a housewife may call her a treasure.
The bread is not sour and the meat does not burn,
　When such faultless hands the buckwheat cakes turn.

In her kitchen is order, and her parlor is neat.
　To be in her company is surely a treat.
She treats all callers as a true lady would,
　And feeds all her guests with pure. wholesome food.

LOVELINESS.

Beautiful scenes so fair and bright
Seen in the dawn and in the light
Beautiful roses. lovely queens
  All through the land of beauty seen,

Lovely maiden so charming and fair,
  Her sweetness of temper we all love to share.
Her graceful form and her red dimpled cheeks.
  Of ease and pleasure they plainly bespeak.

Lovely flowers that bloom in the spring,
  Beautiful birds that merrily sing,
Majestic forests looking aloft,
  Downy pillow white and soft,

Love that is born of the soul pure and deep,
  Never is idle nor lazily sleeps;
Constant and true what e'er may betide,
  Always seeking the true and upright.

THE FOREST

I love to see the stately pine
  Sway in the stormy breeze;
And hear the sighing of the winds
  Which oft the ear does please.

I love to see the sturdy oak
 Its powerful branches spread;
Affording shelter from the heat,
  Or from the rain instead.

The lordly beach and powerful elm
  Come boldly forth to view,
And give us shelter from the wind,
  As well as firewood too.

The forests of this mighty globe,
  Do untold wealth possess,
They're used for building everywhere
  And easy of access.

They build our cottage by the sea
  Or on the lone hillside;
They build our ships of untold worth,
  Which breast the angry tide.

SELF RELIANCE.

We must on ourselves rely,
  And our minds with force apply;
Work with hand, with head and heart:
  They are all, of us a part.

Listen not to people's talk,
  Lest you follow in their walk;
And when they their end have gained,
  Their advice, you'll find was feigned.

People who have wealth and fame,
  Oft' despise an humble name:
Gold and silver's all they crave,
  Making poor men unto slaves.

If misfortune's open paws
  Should attack you with its claws,
Labor on from day to day,
  And with honor, clear the way.

Brave the tempest and the storm,
  Though of earthly treasures shorn.
If you do the best you can,
  Surely that becomes a man.

Self reliance is a boon,
  Never makes a man a loon;
Men of greatness have depended
  On their talents, they expended.

THE WANDERER.

He left his home, so cosy and snug,
  To see the world at its best;
He eagerly sought and at last he did sigh.
  For nowhere could he find rest.

At home he had comfort, pleasure and ease,
  Kind parents, good neighbors and friends;
Yet he leaves all behind to see other lands,
  Where his earthly goods freely he spends.

He buys a ticket to go to New York,
  Or one to the far golden west;
He wants to be cowboy and dash o'er the plains,
  For he thinks that all cowboys are blest.

When he gets to the city, if money he has,
  He tries to cut a big dash,
Where confidence men are friendly to him
  As long as he has any cash.

When he gets on the prairies and sees the wide plains,
  His poor aching heart fills with dread;
He cries in despair as the mantle of night,
  Its ghostly gloom o'er him spreads.

Yet he perseveres on, for roam he must,
  Whether tramp or beggar or king
And oft' by himself in a grave lonesome nook,
  The pleasures of home he will sing.

DUTY

Be merry and gay
And ne'er go astray
While here upon earth we must tarry;
Be kind to your beau
And others you know
And blest be the day when you marry.

Attend to your duty
For there is much beauty
In this great land far and wide;
There's much work to be done
'Neath this hot glowing sun,
Then all work with honor and pride.

Nay never be weary
Though days may be dreary
And filled with much sorrow and care;
Then fling away sorrow
And look to the morrow
For then we may joys fully share.

Be content with your station
And help your relation
And friends that are kind good and true
Kind words that are spoken
Is surely a token
Of hearts that are loving and true.

In this wide world of fame
Some oft gain a name
That's remembered for ages to come;
Though financially poor
Their thoughts were pure
Which in a straight channel did run.

But the reaper soon cometh
And a doleful tune hummeth
He spares neither brambles nor grain:
His book he will open
And reward with a token
All those who are worthy the same.

OBSERVE.

Far over the mountains, rivers and lea,
  Where the forests are reaching out to the sea,
Where ships are landed from far distant climes
  And jolly old sailors are having good times,

Far down in that country is always sunshine.
  No snow storms nor ice, for the weather is fine.
There are sweet-scented flowers that are wafted on air,
  Where flowers are blooming and roses are fair.

Way up in the north where no ice fetters break,
  Where the winds bloweth chill and make a man shake;
There the sun never shines and the roses ne'er bloom.
  Sure, that is a country o'ershadowed with gloom.

Betwixt and between in the north temperate zone,
  All busy people will never be lone.
We have summer and autumn, winter and spring,
  Where beautiful birds, their daily song sing.

We have mighty big forests spread all over this land,
  An intelligent people, who in freedom do stand.
We have wealth that's unbounded, much gold and alloy,
  Where all may with pleasure, this short life enjoy.

HAPPINESS.

How happy and gay
Are the children at play,

For they know not of sorrow nor care.
How cheerful and merry
To amusements they hurry,
For each wants to get her full share.

How eager to learn
When to study they turn
Though the school room has charms for the few.
Yet their master will teach
If the top they would reach
They must work or they'll never get through.

How pleasant to roam
In the woodland at home,
Where the flowers remind us of spring,
With a fair young love
Like a gentle dove,
Who With joy to each other will cling.

How happy are they,
Who, at work or at play.
Their duty with honor fulfill;
Who are gentle and kind
To all of mankind,
And bear to each other good will.

WORK.

Work is honest and must be done.
Idleness always carefully shun;
Work with a will and work with your might,
For work is an honor, if always done right.

Work neath the sun as the day passes by,
Never give vent to a moan or a sigh;
Work in the morn and work in the eve,
For unto work prosperity cleaves.

Work is always wherever we go,
So we all the good seed of labor should sow,
For work we must with head and with hand,
And cultivate all this broad fertile land.

'Tis work that sows the grain on our soil,
While beautiful dames in the kitchen must toil;
'Tis work that builds our cities and towns,
While skillful hands must make women's gowns.

'Tis work in all departments of life,
To win fame and honor we must honestly strive;
For those who are honest and work with a will,
Will come out with success at the top of the hill.

We see those before us who the top long have reached,
And who unto the people salvation have preached;
While those who once labored to gain daily bread,
Yet rose, and with power, this nation have led.

DEPENDENCE.

There once was a man who always depended,
  And as you will see, his life sadly ended;
No effort in life he tried to put forth
  And thus he died in shame and remorse.

What anyone told him he carelessly done,
  For a will of his own he surely had none:
He was dirty and ragged and never was clean
  For all that he done was disgusting and mean.

He played at all games and often did win,
  Yet he never thought he committed a sin;
He smoked, he drank, he stole and he lied;
  And every time the truth he denied.

He often was drunk and picked up from the street,
  Yet to all good advice he never took heed;
His once many friends all deserted him now,
  For the fiend of the wicked was wrote on his brow.

He is old and he's wretched and full of despair,
  In madness and rage he is tearing his hair;
He taketh a dagger and endeth his life
  To land in eternity, misery and strife.

WHEN WE'LL BE FREE.

A few more days we wearily must toil
And gain a living from this earthly soil;
A short abode in this vain glorious world
  Until eternity our banner's will unfurl.

In bondage and temptation here we tread
  Our mortal frame will soon be with the dead;
No freedom here while this short life remains
  For human flesh is full of aches and pains.

A few more years the harvest we must reap
  A few more nights engaged in restless sleep;
All quickly passing onward to the goal
  While making grave atonement for a single soul.

When in that bright eternity at last we dwell
  Where everlasting pleasure and everything is well,
Shall cheer this weary mind though oft amiss
  Which soon abides in happiness and bliss.

ASPIRATION.

After noble things we all should aspire,
  And leave all the vile things of earth;
For nature is kind in shedding abroad
  Those beauties to which she gave birth.

We should all aspire to honor and fame,
  In truth we should work with our might;
For never in life will we need to complain
  If we do that which always is right.

Respect and good will we to others should bear
  For a true heart ne'er hatred will cherish;
A heart full of passion, hatred and lust
  In the end will most certainly perish.

Fair dealing with all the rich and the poor
  Is essential to men of success;
And those who would rise to honor and fame
  Must be true to all, nothing less.

No matter what labor, profession, or trade.
  We should all do the best that we can;
So be gentle and kind, polite and upright
  Which belongs to a woman or man.

A BUMBLEBEE.

Harmless little birdie,
  Said the youthful child,
I am bound to catch you,
  Though you are so wild.

In the blooming clover,
  Buzzing blithe and free,
I must sure possess him
  And hold him just a wee.

Little child, so merry,
  Catches him at last;
Holds him for a moment,
  And throws him down so fast.

Though the bee was pretty,
  It was hot as blaze;
For it stung its captor
  In his hands and face.

The stings were very painful,
  They swelled so fast and hard,
And the youthful child was sorry,
  Because it was so smart.

BEAUTY

Beauty may everywhere be found,
  By those who truly seek it;
'Tis in the heavens and the earth,
  While nature plain bespeaks it.

There's beauty in the moon and stars
  That shine on deep dark nights;
There's beauty in the morning sun
  That gives us warmth and light.

The verdure of the fields and woods
  Are clothed in beauty's way;
The flowers, that bloom in all the land,
  Have charms that will always stay.

Some birds are clothed with beauty rare,
  That sing about our door;
The waves of ocean have this charm,
  As they dash against the shore.

The human family is much endowed
  With grace, with love and beauty:
This faculty will never lack
  To do its bounded duty.

RECOLLECTIONS OF CHILDHOOD.

Those pleasant scenes of childhood, I never can forget,
And as I think them over, it often makes me fret;
The precious time I wasted, and foolishly did spend,
Which is so fast and fleeting, and is only to us lent.

Those old familiar scenes come up before my gaze.
On my mind they are imprinted, that time cannot efface.
The homestead and the farm yard, the woodland and the glen,
Where oft' I sat so musingly, and listened to the wren.

The old familiar pathway, that led us to the stream,
Where oft' we went a' fishing, and of higher thoughts we'd dream;
The woodland ,too, is dearer for the flowers we gathered there,
Though the woodland long has changed into meadow bright and fair.

The quarrels and disputes we had, while cutting off the corn.
And how we'd cry and shiver on a cold hard frosty morn,
When out to dig potatoes before the sun was up
And late within the evening dusk our mush and milk we'd sup.

To gather nuts in autumn time, we never would delay,
    But rose at morn quite early and soon were on our way
Out to the shady forest, where nuts were falling fast,
    Where we all were so contented and forgot the troubled past.

In the long cold winter evenings, I well remember now,
    How many pleasant times we spent, yet some times had a row,
Around the fire we used to sit and learn to read and spell,
    And listen to goblin stories our parents used to tell.

RAMBLER'S KANSAS RAMBLINGS.

In Kansas, one summer, I rambled
Among the corn and the hay.
I hired out to a farmer of merit,
And there I intended to stay.

I was sad, dejected and weary,
From four days' ride in the train;
I was dusty and my purse was quite airy,
So from luxuries I had to refrain.

For three days I wielded an axe,
Which was rather hard on my frame.
The wood was so tough and wiry
But I worked hard to get all the game.

I was glad to follow the plow
In the bottom near by the old creek;
Where was timber, and birds were a' singing
And frogs by the waters did leap.

I plowed there for nearly a month,
And the rich soil over I turned;
The corn-stalks, I cut with a sulky,
And laid in the shade 'neath the ferns.

The creek was timbered and shady
By trees that grew on its banks;
When the heat was oppressive and sultry,
There were grumblers, growlers and cranks.

The rabbits and gophers were plenty,
　In the bushes they played hide and seek,
The serpents neither were backward
　But came forth with a good deal of cheek.

The corn they put in with a planter
　That checked two rows at a time;
The machine was drawn by two horses,
　And the wire kept up a dim chime.

Next the cultivating season came round
　And a sulky of course I did ride;
This too was drawn by two horses
　So I worked with a great deal of pride.

The corn it grew very fast,
　And soon we were all hid from view;
So I rested and wrote out some verses,
　But the verses were slim and quite few.

The gentle breeze always was welcome
　To relieve the heat of the day;
The worker and traveler alike were
　Inclined to be merry and gay.

The "prairie grass" served us for hay
　Which was cut and stacked in a heap;
While snakes and varmints and insects
　Went lazily there to sleep.

The house dog grew lazy and snappish
 As the days became sultry with heat;
But boys who were to go bare-foot,
 Sought shoes to put on their feet.

The grapes and mulberries ripened
 And bore some two hundred fold;
So on Sunday us boys we would go there
 And eat them as stories we told.

Of plums there was an abundance
 Which grew down by the old stream;
Of strawberries we ate a good many
 Put down with sugar and cream.

Some trees they were loaded with cherries
 That sparkled out in the bright sun;
When "Harry" and I did pick them
 Together we had lots of fun.

The apples were very delicious
 Which Harry hauled into the town;
And many a time I did watch him
 When he acted like a comic old clown.

Next Harry and I in the wheat field
 Lay plots to have a good time;
And among us we argued the question
 As to who could compose the best rhyme.

We hauled our wheat in a wagon
  And put into big stacks:
We worked hard till night was a' coming
  With our frail weary boies all racked.

On sunday I'd oft' go to church
  Where a woman the gospel revealed;
And told them of things that's eternal,
  While nothing from them she concealed.

A man he would preach at intervals,
  And tell them of drunkards and hell;
He denounced those that carried the bottle,
  And spoke of those who had fell.

The vast boundless prairie is charming,
  Has a wondrous fascinating spell;
And the true pioneers who first went there
  Of hardships many a story can tell.

The "Red-skins" have long since departed
  Where civilization now ~~grows~~ Grows;
The soil is rich and quite fertile
  'Tis pleasure there to repose

WORLDLY GAIN.

Remember friends, that worldly gain
　　Have many brought to grief;
For worldly pleasures all are vain,
　　That here you can receive,

Though countless wealth of gold you stow
　　Away in yonder vault,
If still your evil seeds you sow,
　　And always are at fault.

'Tis well enough that we should strive
　　For grand success in life,
And always do our very best
　　With will, and power and might.

Be cautious then about your gain,
　　And use it for the best:
That when you from this world depart
　　You may forever rest.

THE FARMER BOY.

The farmer boy must work all day.
  In summer time he rakes the hay,
And stirs up wasps and bumble-bees
  Which sting him on his baggy knees.

On rainy days he's out to fish,
  Or gets into some fruit some dish
And eats away with might and main
  And wishes it would always rain.

When hoeing corn out in the field
  He seeks a shade tree for his shield,
He falls asleep and snores away
  Until he hears the dinner horn play.

He like's the pies that mother bakes
  And eats the frosting off the cakes:
He's always on the quick lookout
  To see if anyone's about.

To dig up 'taters makes him sad:
  When husking corn he feels quite bad;
When Sunday comes he's bright and gay
  And all day long he spends in play.

Yea, truly he's not always sad
  He's merry when he fishe's for shad;
And oh how happy when the pies
  Upon the table meet his eyes.

In winter he's contented quite,
  When cracking nuts by the chimney light
And pleased when skating he can go
  Which sets boys faces all aglow.

TEMPTATIONS.

Temptations are numerous: they are offered **day** by day
To the innocent and virtuous as they travel on their way
They catch the youth unwary in their foul and filthy snare.
And laugh with fiendish horror, as their number swells with care.

'Tis whiskey, wine and brandy, they seem so neat and gay
And with cheerful glowing colors they beckon you that way;
So when they've got you fully, to tread the downward road,
The old tempter laughs and scorns you, and o'er your misery gloats.

From bad to worse he leads you till the drama is complete.
He shapes his worldly pleasures in a manner strange and neat.
With cute devices cunning, the virtuous he baits,
While from his secret hiding place, in eagerness he **waits**.

THOUGHTFULNESS.

From humble spheres we rise to fame,
    While honor from this this world we gain,
A thought may spring into an act
    In years to come become afact.

Twa's thoughtfulness that made the cranks
    And filled their minds with curious pranks
They made the lightening message speed
    Like lightening on a furious stee l

The inventor gave himself to thought,
    And thereby gained his happy lot
The genius also won his fame
    By thoughtfulness when he was sane.

The genius oft is called a crank
    Because he's wise among his rank:
Yet superstitious people say,
    He had no reason in his day.

HOME.

Have you thought of home and its beautiful charms?
    Have you thought of those loved ones, so dear,
Or have you forgotten the times round the hearth,
    Where we gathered when winter was drear?

We often look back to that once happy time.
    Which in pleasure and peace we did spend.
Those were moments of joy, of pleasure and bliss,
    While many dear friends we now sadly miss.

When from sisters, brothers and parents you go,
    You will oft find the world very heartless and cold;
You can scarce find a friend who your troubles will share,
    Then for your own self and welfare must take care.

Oh! beautiful home, a picture so rare,
  Where peace and contentment shall know no despair,
Where everything in harmony flows,
  Where all is peace as time onward goes.

No other place in this world can you find,
  Where people like brothers and sisters are kind.
If you find a friend, be sure he is true,
  For many false ones will flock around you.

If you are rich, do not poor men despise,
  To display all your wealth is surely not wise,
For many in a lowly thatched cottage were born,
  Yet rose to great wealth in life's early morn.

Many great men were born of parents quite poor,
  But the influence of home made their wisdom secure.
So despise not your home, my fine little lad,
  Though the frowns of some people may make you feel sad.

Home should be a place of love and of peace,
  Of happiness, pleasure, contentment and ease.
Do then home not despise, though homely it be,
  For great men from humble homes rose as you see.

THE FARMER.

The farmer, how contented he must be
As he lives on his farm so happy and free.
With naught to disturb him when the day's work is over
But to look o'er his fields of bright blooming clover.

His cattle are sleek and all so well fed
That he never despairs or troubles his head
About grave misfortunes that never may come,
But sits down with ease and counts up his sum.

As the seasons come 'round he is merry and gay;
He is very ambitious and works through the day,
For he knows that his labors will be crowned with success
And on that assurance he goes to his rest.

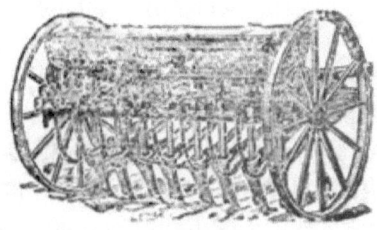

He plants his potatoes and also his corn.
  He hustles around and works in the morn.
He sows his oats on the drear barren ground
  Where an unusual rich harvest in the fall will be found.

When haying comes 'round he is out very early.
  He is quite contented and scarce ever surly.
He cuts the clover and lays the grass low,
  While the gentle breeze blows through his hair to and fro.

'Tis a pleasure for him when he goes out to drive.
  To see others like him, abundantly thrive.
and thus many days in pleasure he spends,
  As he through the green forests his way homeward wends.

The time for corn husking soon will be here.
   And he sees his success as he pulls up the ears;
He fills up his cribs some two hundred-fold
   To feed to his stock when the winter is cold.

Soon the bleak winds of winter will sweep o'er the moor,
   And leave many wanderers, homeless and poor,
Who did not work any through the long summer days,
   But in idleness wandered from place unto place.

When winter comes 'round, by his fireside warm,
   He knows he is safe from the fierce raging storm,
And takes consolation in the work he has done
   'Neath the bright blue sky and the hot blazing sun.

    The farmer works and tills the soil
      Fron morn' till eve' it's honest toil.

    He sows his seed and reaps his grain;
      From it he lives, the matter's plain.

At noon he rests beneath the shade
  Though oft' his labor's illy paid;
Yet independent he may be,
  For from depending ties he's free.

In winter when the cold wind blows,
  He has wholesome comfort; this he knows,
As around his warm fireside he sits,
  And watches wife and children knit.

He raises fruit and garden truck.
  To sell his wares he's oft' in luck.
He labors while the bright sun shines,
  And at his sumptuous table dines.

Of course he must toil and work, this we know,
  And oft' he has sorrow, trouble and woe:
Adversity sometimes may fall to his lot,
  And then for a time this bright scene is forgot.

DO YOUR DUTY.

If a task is once begun,
Work until the crown is won;
   Sit not idly in the shade.
Stir the soil with hoe or spade.
   See what others done before.
This you can and maybe more.

All your wants you should supply.
   This you can if you will try.
Always lend a helping hand.
   As you wander through this land
For we all can useful be
   In this land among the free.

Anything, though great or small.
   Never falter lest you fall.
If you would to honor rise.
   Do not little things despise.
For the littles by-and-by
   Build a temple to the sky.

www.ingramcontent.com/pod-product-compliance
Lightning Source LLC
Chambersburg PA
CBHW030857260626
47169CB00008B/2577